RAINBOW JOE AND ME

Maria Diaz Strom

LEE & LOW BOOKS, Inc. • New York

Printed in Hong Kong by South China Printing Co. (1988) Ltd.

Book Design by Christy Hale
Book Production by The Kids at Our House

The text is set in Myriad Tilt
The illustrations are rendered in acrylic on bristol board

10 9 8 7 6 5 4 3 2 1
First Edition

Library of Congress Cataloging-in-Publication Data
Strom, Maria Diaz.
Rainbow Joe and Me / written and illustrated by Maria Diaz Strom. — 1st ed.
p.   cm.
Summary: Eloise shares her love of colors with her blind friend Rainbow Joe,
who makes his own colors when he plays beautiful notes on his saxophone.
ISBN 1-880000-93-8 (hardcover)
[1. Color Fiction.   2. Blind Fiction.   3. Physically handicapped Fiction.
4. Saxophone Fiction.   5. Music Fiction.]   I. Title.
PZ7.S9216Ra   1999
[E]—dc21   99-25585
                                                             CIP   AC

To my students at the Texas School for the Blind and
Visually Impaired, who inspired me to write this book.

And to my loving husband, Jay Margolis,
who showed me the music of New Orleans.—M.D.S.

my name is Eloise and I make colors.
I mix up red and white and make fish.
Crazy pink fish swimming across my
paper. I mix up red and blue and make
monkeys. Purple monkeys swinging
high in yellow trees.

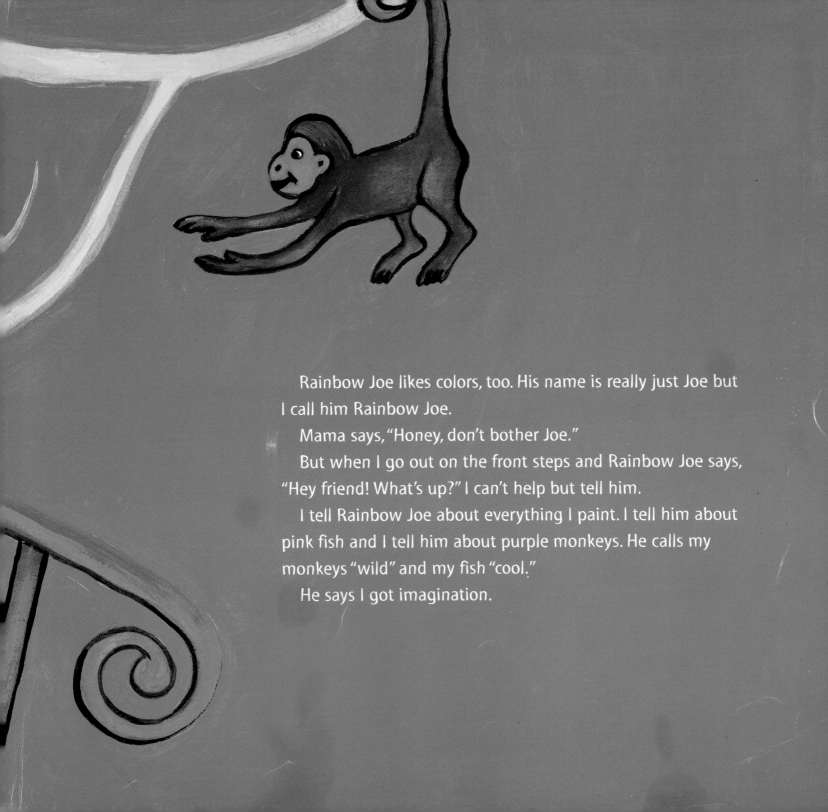

Rainbow Joe likes colors, too. His name is really just Joe but I call him Rainbow Joe.

Mama says, "Honey, don't bother Joe."

But when I go out on the front steps and Rainbow Joe says, "Hey friend! What's up?" I can't help but tell him.

I tell Rainbow Joe about everything I paint. I tell him about pink fish and I tell him about purple monkeys. He calls my monkeys "wild" and my fish "cool."

He says I got imagination.

Rainbow Joe says he can make colors, too. But he can't see with his eyes like me. Rainbow Joe says he sees colors inside his head. I ask him, "How are you going to mix those colors?"

Rainbow Joe hums and taps his feet. "Eloise," he says, "I got my own special way with colors. I know how to make them sing. One of these days I'm going to show you."

Mama calls me to come inside and I tell her about Rainbow Joe making colors. But Mama says, "Honey, a blind man can't mix colors. They'll turn out all gray like this dishwater."

I go back to painting. I paint olive elephants and maroon
monsters. I see Rainbow Joe on the steps and I tell him
about mixing up black and yellow to make olive,
and purple and red to make maroon.

He says, "I've been mixing up something,
too. Just for you, Eloise."

"Show me."

"You'll see," he says.

Then he leans his head back and says, "I see yellow, Eloise. Yellow's like butter melting on your tongue.

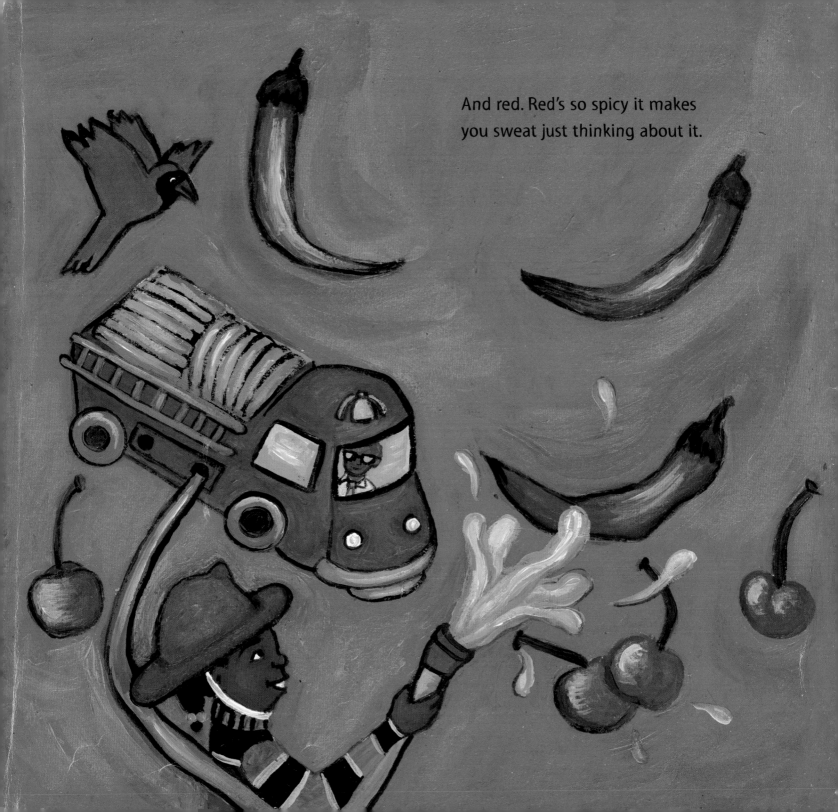

And red. Red's so spicy it makes you sweat just thinking about it.

And green. Sweet gr-e-e-e-e-n. That's a color so soft you just want to lie down in it and take a nap."

Rainbow Joe says he likes blue best. When he talks about blue I can tell he's really seeing. "Bah-bah-bah-blue!" He taps his feet and shakes his head. "There's a whole lot a blue in this world," he says.

Some days I go to see Rainbow Joe and I take my paint and paper with me. Rainbow Joe tells me about the old days. I paint what he tells me.

I ask him, "You going to show me how you mix colors?"

He says, "I'll show you someday, Eloise."

I can't wait.

Mama calls and I go inside.

I can't stop wondering about how Rainbow Joe mixes colors. Does he use a brush like me? I close my eyes and pick up my brush. My brush touches color. But which one? I can't see. My brush touches down again. I don't know where, but I start mixing colors. In my mind I see orange snakes slithering on green grass. I mix and I paint and I open my eyes.

I see gray. A big gray blob. I think
for a minute that maybe Mama
was right. Maybe Rainbow Joe can't
mix colors. But then I remember
melted butter and spicy red and I
believe that he's going to paint me
a great big beautiful picture someday.

One Sunday morning, Mama and I are leaving for church and there he is. Sitting on the steps, humming and tapping his feet, just like always. But he's got a big brown bag.

"What's in the bag, Rainbow Joe?" I say.

"Been working on my surprise for you, Eloise," he says. "Today I'm going to show you my colors."

Mama takes my hand. "We have to go, Joe. We'll see you after church," she says.

I wonder what's in that bag. All through church I squiggle and squirm. Mama tells me to keep still, but I can't.

Finally church is over. We shake the reverend's hand on the way out, but all I can think about is my surprise.

As soon as we get to our block I let go of Mama's
hand and I run to Rainbow Joe. He opens up the bag
and pulls out an old saxophone.

"This is for you, Eloise," he says.

He starts to blow. Colors fly. Big strong red notes
and little yellow notes. Rainbow Joe mixes them
up to make bright orange. He blows
deep blue notes and holds them in
the air for a long time. Then green.
Long, lazy green. Then violet.
Pretty violet that blends
back into blue.

Mama and I listen to the colors.
We tap our feet and clap our hands.
Rainbow Joe mixes up a great big
beautiful rainbow. And we see
every color. We see it all!